It's Fun to Be Five

It's Fun to Be Five

A
LITTLE APPLE
PAPERBACK

SCHOLASTIC INC.
New York   Toronto   London   Auckland   Sydney
Mexico City   New Delhi   Hong Kong

12 11 10 9 8 7 6 5 4 3 2   0 1 2 3 4 5/0
                                                 23

Printed in the U.S.A.
First Scholastic printing, February 2000

Table of Contents

Introduction

You're five? Lucky you! There are so many things you can do now that you are five — things you were too young to do just last year, when you were only four. Now that you are five you can go to kindergarten, make new friends, and even camp out in a tent!

In this book you'll find eight stories about five-year-olds. Timothy is just starting school. Junie B. Jones has a new baby brother. Olivia and Rachel Parker are best friends who do not always get along. Franklin is a five-year-old who worries that his best friend is growing up faster than he is. Frog and Toad are best friends who like to tell each other how they feel. Grace is a five-year-old who has big dreams, and Wendy is a five-year-old witch!

No matter what is happening, every five-year-old you'll read about knows that even though there might be some scary moments, being five is, most of all, very, very fun!

It's Fun to Be Five

From

JUNIE B. JONES AND A LITTLE MONKEY BUSINESS

by Barbara Park

Junie B. Jones often speaks before she thinks and sometimes lands in a lot of trouble. In this story, Junie has misunderstood something her grandmother said and she's told all her classmates that her baby brother is a real, live monkey. Nobody believes her, so Junie gets mad and ends up in the principal's office.

The school office is a scary place.

It has loud ringing phones. And a typing lady who is a stranger. And a row of chairs where bad kids sit.

Mrs. plopped me in a blue one.

"Wait here," she said.

"Yeah, only I'm not bad," I whispered to just myself.

Then I put my sweater on my head. So nobody would see me in the bad kid's chair.

After that, I peeked down my long sweater sleeve. And I saw Mrs. out of my hand hole. She was knocking on Principal's door.

Then she went in there. And my heart felt very pumpy. Because she was tattle-taling on me, I think.

After a while, she came out again. Principal came with her.

Principal has a baldy head which looks like rubber.

Also, he has big hands. And heavy shoes. And a suit made out of black.

"Could I see you in my office for a minute, Junie B.?" he said.

And so then I had to go in there all by myself. And I sat in a big wood chair. And Principal made me take the sweater off my head.

"So what's this all about?" he said. "Why do you think your teacher brought you down here today?"

"Because," I said very quiet.

"Because why?" said Principal.

"Because that Grace shot off her

big fat mouth," I explained.

Then Principal folded his arms. And he said for me to start at the beginning.

And so I did. . . .

First, I told him about how I spent the night at my grampa's house.

"We had delicious waffles for breakfast," I said. "And I had five of them. Only my grampa didn't know where I put them all. Except I put them way in here."

Then I opened my mouth and showed Principal where my waffles went.

After that, I told him how my grandma Miller came home from the hospital. And she told me I had a monkey brother. For really and honest and truly.

"And so then I told the children at Show and Tell," I said. "And at recess Lucille and that Grace started giving me lots of pretty stuff. Because they wanted to be first to see him.

"Except too bad for me," I said. "Because when we came inside, Mrs. found out about the snack tickets. And then that dumb Grace shot off her big fat mouth about her shoes. And so I got marched down here. And I had to sit in the bad kid's chair."

Then I smoothed my skirt. "The end," I said nicely.

Principal rubbed his head that looks like rubber.

"Junie B., maybe we should go back to when your grandmother came home from the hospital," he said. "Can you remember *exactly* what she said about your brother being a monkey?"

I scrunched my eyes real tight to remember.

"Yes," I said. "Grandma Miller

said he was the cutest little monkey she ever saw."

Then Principal closed his eyes. "Aaah," he said kind of quiet. "Now I get it."

After that, he smiled a little bit. "You see, Junie B., when your grandmother called your brother a little monkey, she didn't mean he was a *real* little monkey. She just meant he was, well . . . cute."

"I know he's cute," I said. "That's because all monkeys are cute. Except for I don't like the big kind that can kill you."

Principal shook his head. "No,

Junie B., that's not what I mean. I mean your brother isn't really a monkey at all. He's just a little baby boy."

I made a frowny face. "No, he is *not* a little baby boy," I told him. "He's a real, alive, baby monkey with black hairy fur and long fingers and toes. You can ask my grandma Miller if you don't believe me."

And so guess what Principal did then? He called her, that's what! He called Grandma Miller right up on the phone!

And then he talked to her. And then I talked to her too!

"Hey, Grandma!" I said very shouty. "Guess what just happened down here? Principal said that my baby brother isn't a real, alive monkey. Only he is. 'Cause you told me that. Remember? You said he was a monkey. For really and honest and truly."

Then Grandma Miller said she was very sorry. But she didn't mean he was a *real* monkey. She just meant he was *cute*.

Just like Principal explained to me.

And so then I felt very droopy inside.

"Yeah, only what about all of his black hair? And his long fingers and toes?" I said. "And what about his bed that looks like a cage? And the wallpaper with his jungle friends on it?"

But Grandma Miller kept on saying that my new brother was just a really cute baby. And so finally I didn't want to talk to her anymore. And I hanged up the phone.

Then I bended my head way down. And my eyes got a little bit of wet in them.

"Darn it," I said very quiet.

After that, Principal gave me a

tissue. And he said, "I'm sorry," to me.

Then he held my hand.

And me and him walked back to Room Nine.

From

TIMOTHY GOES TO SCHOOL

by Rosemary Wells

Not everything new is fun right away. In this story, Timothy has a hard time starting school, until he meets a friend who helps him see how much fun it can be.

"I'm never going back to school," said Timothy.

"Why not?" called his mother.

"Because Claude is the smartest and the best at everything and he has all the friends," said Timothy.

"You'll feel better in your new football shirt," said Timothy's mother.

Timothy did not feel better in his
new football shirt.

That morning Claude played the
saxophone.
"I can't stand it anymore," said a
voice next to Timothy.

It was Violet.

"You can't stand what?" Timothy asked Violet.

"Grace!" said Violet. "She sings. She dances. She counts up to a thousand and she sits next to me!"

During playtime Timothy and Violet stayed together.

Violet said, "I can't believe you've

been here all along!"

"Will you come home and have cookies with me after school?" Timothy asked.

On the way home Timothy and
Violet laughed so much about
Claude and Grace that they both
got the hiccups.

From

THE WITCH WHO WAS AFRAID
OF WITCHES

by Alice Low

Wendy is the youngest witch in her family. She has a hard time proving to her older sisters that she's big enough to join them in their witchy frolics. Besides, she's a little afraid of them. And to make things worse, she's lost her magic broomstick. But maybe, just maybe, things will change on Halloween.

On Halloween night, her sisters said, "We are going to the city where there are more people to scare."

"Take me with you," Wendy said. "Please."

"Really, Wendy, how can you come with us when you have no broomstick?" her oldest sister said.

"Can't I ride with you on yours?" Wendy asked.

"Of course not. You would make it too heavy. Stay here, and don't let anyone in. All those trick-or-treaters eat our candy and squirt shaving cream on the rug. Remember, don't let them in."

Wendy wasn't afraid of trick-or-treaters. She was much more afraid of witches.

"Turn off the lights, lock the door, and put out the fire," her oldest sister said. "It will look like nobody is home."

Wendy did as they said.

Then she sat in the dark, shivering. If only she had her broomstick for company.

Soon there was a knock on the door.

"Trick or treat," shouted a voice. Wendy opened the door and called out, "There's nobody home."

"You're home," said a small ghost on the doorstep.

"Well, I'm nobody," Wendy said.

"Is that what you are for Halloween?" asked the ghost. "Are you nobody?"

"Yes," Wendy said. "But I'm dressed as a witch."

"Well, why don't you come trick-or-treating with me?" asked the ghost. "My best friend, Billy, went trick-or-treating with his other best friend, who doesn't like me. Let's follow them and scare them."

"That sounds good to me," Wendy said. "Though I'm not very good at scaring people. Mostly, *I'm* scared of witches."

"Oh, you'll catch on," said the ghost. "You just go woo, woo, woo."

"That's how *ghosts* go," Wendy said. "Witches cackle. Like this. *Heh, heh, heh. I'll get you.*"

"Very good," said the ghost. "You sound like a real witch."

"Do I?" Wendy said. "I never

thought I could cackle before. But I can't be a real witch without a broomstick. I lost mine."

"Oh, if that's all you need, we have an old one at home. Come on."

They walked up a long path to the ghost's house.

The ghost's mother gave Wendy hot chocolate and a candied apple and a broomstick.

Wendy thought it would be nice to stay there all evening, instead of flying around scaring people.

But the ghost said, "Get on. Let's see you ride."

"I'm not any good at riding

broomsticks," Wendy said, afraid to try. "I have no witch power."

"Take the broomstick anyway," said the ghost.

So Wendy took the broomstick, but she didn't sit on it. This old kitchen broomstick wouldn't give her any witch power.

"Go on," said the ghost. "Sit on it. It's fun."

"Okay," Wendy said. After all, the ghost didn't expect her to do anything but pretend and have fun.

She sat on the broomstick and said, *"Heh, heh, heh. I'll get you."* Then she gave a little jump.

She took off so fast she hit the ceiling and fell down.

The ghost was amazed. So was the ghost's mother.

"That must be a magic broomstick," said the ghost. "Here, let me try it."

The ghost got on and said, "Heh, heh, heh. I'll get you." Then he gave a little jump.

But nothing happened.

"Darn it. It doesn't work," said the ghost.

"I'll try it," said the ghost's mother.

She sat on it and cackled and gave

a little jump.

But nothing happened again.

They were both very disappointed.

"I'll try it again," Wendy said.

Again, she took off easily. But this time, she zoomed around and around before she landed.

"I guess I do have a little witch power," she said.

"I never thought so before. Except I don't know any spells."

"Then make one up," said the ghost. "You're magic."

That made a really good spell pop into Wendy's head. She said it, in a frightening voice.

> *Frogs and lizards*
> *Toads and newts*
> *Rubbers, raincoats*
> *Hiking boots.*
> *Turn this ghost*
> *Into a witch.*
> *Presto, change-o*
> *Make a switch.*

The ghost's robes turned black. "Great!" said the ghost. "I wanted to be a witch, but we didn't have any black sheets. But I need a pointed hat."

"Oh, that's easy," Wendy said. "I don't even have to think about that one."

Stew and brew
And cat and bat.
Give this witch
A pointed hat.

"Great!" said the new witch, touching the pointed hat on his head. "Now let's fly out the window."

"Be careful," said the new witch's mother. "Don't fly too fast."

"We won't," they called from the broomstick as they flew out, with Wendy steering.

First they swooped over trees and made the leaves fall off.

Next they swooped over cars and scared the drivers.

Then they swooped into the party where Billy and his best friend were ducking for apples.

Billy and his best friend were so scared, they ran home crying.

When the clock struck midnight, Wendy said, "I'd better fly you home."

"I want to come home with you and keep on being a witch," said the new witch. "You *are* a real witch, aren't you?"

"Yes, I am a real witch," Wendy said. "With my own witch power. I just found that out, and you helped. But I have to turn you back into a ghost and take you home. Your mother would miss you."

> *Broiled figs*
> *And toasted toast.*
> *Turn this witch*
> *Back to a ghost.*

The new witch became a ghost again, in his own kitchen.

The ghost's mother let Wendy keep the broomstick.

"Thanks a lot," Wendy said. "See you next Halloween."

And she flew home and went to sleep without worrying about witches. She wasn't afraid of witches anymore.

From

THE BIG ALFIE OUT OF DOORS STORYBOOK

by Shirley Hughes

5

Alfie is five years old, and he's ready to try new things — like camping out in his dad's old tent!

Annie Rose was too little to go camping, so it was going to be just Alfie and Dad. They had brought proper foam mattresses and sleeping bags with them from home.

"I hope it doesn't rain," said Dad.

Alfie could hardly wait until bedtime. He kept going in and out

of the tent to check that everything
was ready. He had put his blanket
and elephant beside his sleeping bag.
Dad had put a flashlight beside his.

At last bedtime came. Alfie had a wash and put on his pajamas and bathrobe just as usual. He wanted to cook his own supper over a camp fire, but Dad said that might be a bit difficult.

Instead they had supper in the kitchen, baked potatoes and baked beans. Grandma gave them some apples to take with them into the tent.

Then they set out. It was strange not to be going upstairs to bed but down the yard, through the gate, and into the field.

It was still light. Dad and Alfie sat down in front of the tent with a blanket around them and ate their apples. They watched the sun go down behind the trees. They watched the sky change color. They saw the birds swooping and calling to one another. They sat there until

it was quite dark and the stars came
out, one by one.

It was very mysterious to be
outside at night under the big sky,
with rustling noises all around and

the wind blowing the branches about. But Alfie felt very safe being there with Dad.

Just before it was time to settle down, Alfie jumped up, scampered off across the field, and did a little dance all by himself under the stars.

Then they climbed into their sleeping bags and Alfie cuddled up to his blanket with his elephant in beside him and went off to sleep.

When he woke up it wasn't morning. It was the middle of the night. It was completely dark, not like being in a bedroom with the light shining in from the landing, but pitch-black all around.

Alfie put out his hand. He could feel Dad's back next to him, humped up inside the sleeping bag. Alfie lay very still and listened. He could hear noises outside, strange creakings and flappings.

Inside the tent he could hear Dad breathing. But then Alfie realized that he could hear something else breathing, too. And that something was *outside the tent*!

Alfie sat up. He didn't scream. He didn't even cry. He just leaned over and wrapped his arms around Dad's neck and squeezed very tightly

indeed. Then, of course, Dad woke
up, too.

Now the
breathing thing
was just near
their heads. It
was a very
snorty, snuffly
sort of breathing.

They could hear it moving, too. It
was trampling about in the grass.
Then it went round the tent to the
zip opening, which Dad had left not
quite done up, and started to push
against it.

Alfie was quite sure that

something huge and horrible was
coming to eat them up. He began to
scream and scream.

"It's okay, Alfie," said Dad. He felt
for his flashlight and switched it on.

They saw a big pink nose coming
through the tent flap. It had very
large wet nostrils.

"It's a pig!" said Dad. And he
bravely got out of his sleeping bag
and gave the nose a big push.

Alfie stopped screaming. He and Dad crawled out of the tent. It did not seem quite so dark outside. The pig moved a short distance away and stood there watching them.

"I didn't know Jim Gatting had put his pig in this field," grumbled Dad sleepily. He tried to make the pig go away, but it wouldn't.

After a while they tried to go back to sleep in the tent, but the pig kept trying to join them.

In the end there was nothing for it but to take the tent down. They collected up all their things and carried them back into Grandma's yard. It took several journeys to and fro. The pig followed closely behind them.

When Dad finally closed the gate on the pig, it stuck its snout through the bars and watched them.

Dad told Alfie that they couldn't very well wake up everybody in the house at that time of night, so they had better put up the tent again in the yard. Alfie thought that was a very good idea.

At last they got the tent back up and crawled into it, and the pig got tired of watching and wandered off down the field.

Alfie and Dad dozed until it was nearly light.

When Alfie woke again, Dad was still fast asleep. Alfie crept quietly out of his sleeping bag and stood in the wet grass in his bare feet. The curtains of Grandma's house were still tightly drawn. But the sun was up and the birds were making a great noise.

Alfie felt very special to be the only person awake and out-of-doors that sunny morning. And he made up his mind to ask Dad if they could go camping again that very night.

From

RACHEL PARKER, KINDERGARTEN SHOW-OFF

by Ann M. Martin

Olivia is very excited when Rachel moves in next door and is in her class. But she feels a little funny because Rachel can do a lot of the things Olivia can do. How can Olivia and Rachel learn to be friends?

At school we have sharing time. Rachel and I sit far apart. We can see each other. I cross my eyes at Rachel. She sticks her tongue out at me.

"Who has something to share?"
asks Mrs. Bee.

Rachel raises her hand. "We are
going to get a cat," she says.

I raise my hand. "*We* already have
a cat," I say.

"That's enough, girls," says Mrs.
Bee.

I shrug my shoulders.

After sharing, Mrs. Bee says,
"Class, today you will have two new
teachers. Their names are Olivia and
Rachel. They will read to you."

Mrs. Bee sits on the floor. She
waits for Rachel and me to choose a
book. Then we fight over Mrs. Bee's
big chair. Guess what — we can fit
in it together.

Rachel begins to read to our class. She reads the first page of the book.

I read the second page.

Uh-oh. Here is a word I do not know. "Mrs. Bee?" I say.

"Mrs. Bee?" my teacher repeats. "Who is that? I do not know any Mrs. Bee. My new name is Alice, and I cannot read yet."

"Oh." I skip over the word. Now the story does not make sense.

Rachel whispers something to me. "It's *jacket*," she says. "That word is *jacket*."

"Thank you," I reply.

On the next page, Rachel gets

stuck on a word. So I whisper it to her.

"Thank you," she replies.

We read the story to the end. When we finish, I smile at Rachel. Maybe she is not such a show-off. Then I say, "Can you come over after school?"

At my house, Rachel and I make a train out of chairs. We pretend to take a trip to Italy.

Then we tie a bonnet on Rosie. We pretend she is our baby.

After that, we pretend we are teachers again.

I read *Little Bear* to Rachel. She reads *The Snowy Day* to me.

"Rachel!" calls Mommy. "Your grandfather wants you to come home now."

"Okay!" Rachel answers. "Olivia, tomorrow you can come to my house."

"And the next day, you can come here again," I say.

"Good-bye, Olivia. I will see you tomorrow."

"Good-bye, Rachel Elizabeth Parker. I am glad you are my friend."

DAYS WITH FROG AND TOAD

by Arnold Lobel

Frog and Toad are best friends. They usually play together every day. But sometimes, even best friends need time apart.

Toad went to Frog's house.

He found a note on the door.

The note said,

"Dear Toad, I am not at home.

I went out.

I want to be alone."

"Alone?" said Toad.

"Frog has me for a friend.
Why does he want to be alone?"

Toad looked through the windows.
He looked in the garden.
He did not see Frog.

Toad went to the woods.

Frog was not there.

He went to the meadow.

Frog was not there.

Toad went down to the river.

There was Frog.

He was sitting on an island

by himself.

"Poor Frog," said Toad.
"He must be very sad.
I will cheer him up."
Toad ran home.
He made sandwiches.
He made a pitcher of iced tea.
He put everything
in a basket.

Toad hurried
back to the river.
"Frog," he shouted,
"it's me.
It's your best friend, Toad!"
Frog was too far away to hear.
Toad took off his jacket

and waved it like a flag.

Frog was too far away to see.

Toad shouted and waved,

but it was no use.

Frog sat on the island.

He did not see or hear Toad.

A turtle swam by.
Toad climbed on the turtle's back.

"Turtle," said Toad,
"carry me to the island.
Frog is there.
He wants to be alone."

"If Frog wants to be alone,"
said the turtle,
"why don't you leave him alone?"

"Maybe you are right," said Toad.
"Maybe Frog does not
want to see me.
Maybe he does not want me
to be his friend anymore."

"Yes, maybe," said the turtle
as he swam to the island.

"Frog!" cried Toad.
"I am sorry for all
the dumb things I do.

I am sorry for all
the silly things I say.
Please be my friend again!"
Toad slipped off the turtle.
With a splash, he fell in the river.

Frog pulled Toad
up onto the island.
Toad looked in the basket.
The sandwiches were wet.
The pitcher of iced tea was empty.

"Our lunch is spoiled," said Toad.
"I made it for you, Frog,
so that you would be happy."

"But Toad," said Frog.
"I *am* happy. I am very happy.
This morning
when I woke up
I felt good because
the sun was shining.

I felt good because
I was a frog.
And I felt good because
I have you for a friend.
I wanted to be alone.
I wanted to think about
how fine everything is."

"Oh," said Toad.
"I guess that is a very good reason

for wanting to be alone."
"Now," said Frog,
"I will be glad *not* to be alone.
Let's eat lunch."

Frog and Toad
stayed on the island
all afternoon.
They ate wet sandwiches
without iced tea.
They were two close friends
sitting alone together.

From

AMAZING GRACE

by Mary Hoffman

Grace has a wonderful imagination, and likes to pretend she is other people. What will happen when Grace has a chance to act out a part that other people don't think she can do?

One day Grace's teacher said they would do the play *Peter Pan*. Grace knew who she wanted to be.

When she raised her hand, Raj said, "You can't be Peter — that's a boy's name."

But Grace kept her hand up.

"You can't be Peter Pan," whispered Natalie. "He isn't black." But Grace kept her hand up.

"All right," said the teacher. "Lots of you want to be Peter Pan, so we'll have auditions next week to choose parts." She gave them words to learn.

When Grace got home, she seemed sad.

"What's the matter?" asked Ma.

"Raj said I can't be Peter Pan because I'm a girl."

"That just shows what Raj knows," said Ma. "A girl can be Peter Pan if she wants to."

Grace cheered up, then later she remembered something else. "Natalie says I can't be Peter Pan because I'm black," she said.

Ma looked angry. But before she could speak, Nana said, "It seems that Natalie is another one who don't know nothing. You can be anything you want, Grace, if you put your mind to it."

On Saturday Nana told Grace they were going out. In the afternoon they caught a bus and train into town. Nana took Grace to a grand theater. The sign outside read ROSALIE WILKINS IN *Romeo and Juliet* in sparkling lights.

"Are we going to the ballet, Nana?" asked Grace.

"We are, honey, but first I want you to look at this picture."

Grace looked up and saw a beautiful young ballerina in a tutu. Above the dancer it said STUNNING NEW JULIET.

"That one is little Rosalie from back home in Trinidad," said Nana. "Her granny and me, we grew up together on the island. She's always asking me do I want tickets to see her Rosalie dance — so this time I said yes."

After the ballet Grace played the

part of Juliet, dancing around her
room in her imaginary tutu. I can
be anything I want, she thought.

On Monday the class met for
auditions to choose who was best
for each part.

When it was Grace's turn to be

Peter, she knew exactly what to do and all the words to say — she had been Peter Pan all weekend. She took a deep breath and imagined herself flying.

When it was time to vote, the class chose Raj to be Captain Hook and Natalie to be Wendy. There was no doubt who would be Peter Pan. *Everyone* voted for Grace.

From

FRANKLIN AND THE TOOTH FAIRY

by Paulette Bourgeois

Franklin and Bear are best friends and have lots in common. But one day, Bear loses his first tooth, and Franklin wonders how he can show he's growing up, too.

Bear showed his tooth to Mr. Owl as soon as he got to school.

Mr. Owl was very excited. "Losing your baby teeth means you are growing up," he said.

Franklin did not say anything. He had no teeth, but he wanted to feel grown-up, too.

Franklin was quiet for the rest of
the day.

Even at home, Franklin was quieter
than usual.

"What's wrong?" asked Franklin's
mother.

"I don't have any teeth," he answered.

"Neither do we," said his father. "That's the way turtles are."

"But I want teeth," said Franklin.

His parents looked surprised.

"My friends get presents from the tooth fairy when they lose their teeth," said Franklin.

"Why do they get presents for old teeth?" asked Franklin's father.

"Because it means they are growing up," said Franklin.

"I see," said his father.

That night, just before bed, Franklin had a good idea. Perhaps

tooth fairies did not know that
turtles have no teeth. He found a
tiny white rock to put under his
shell.

He asked his mother to help him write a note. It read:

Dear Tooth Fairy,

This is a turtle tooth. You may not have seen one before. Please leave a present.

Franklin

Franklin woke up very early the next morning. He looked under his shell. The rock was gone, but there was a note instead of a present.

He ran to his parents' room. "What does it say?" he asked.

Franklin's father put on his reading glasses.

Dear Franklin,

Sorry. Turtles don't have teeth.
Good try.

Your friend, The Tooth Fairy

Franklin was very unhappy until he noticed a big wrapped package near his breakfast bowl.

"Open it," said Franklin's mother.

Inside was a beautiful book.

"Who is it from?" asked Franklin.

"From us," said his parents. "To celebrate your growing up."

Franklin stood very tall. "Thank you."

From then on, Franklin didn't worry about being different from Bear. He knew that, in all the important ways, he and Bear were exactly the same.